To Eric, Bobbie, and everyone at The Eric Carle Museum—
always worth the drive.

Text and illustrations copyright © 2012 by Mo Willems.
ELEPHANT & PIGGIE is a trademark of The Mo Willems Studio, Inc.

This special edition was printed for Kohl's Department Stores, Inc. (for distribution on behalf of Kohl's Cares, LLC, its wholly owned subsidiary), by Hyperion Books for Children, an imprint of Disney Book Group, New York.

Kohl's
Style Number 978-1-368-00972-0
Factory Number 211019
2/17–4/17

First Edition, October 2012
ISBN 978-1-368-00972-0

Printed in Malaysia
Reinforced binding
Library of Congress Cataloging-in-Publication Data on file.

This book is set in Century 725/Monotype; Grilled Cheese BTN/Fontbros; Neutraface, Fink, Typography of Coop/House Industries

Visit hyperionbooksforchildren.com
and pigeonpresents.com

Let's Go for a Drive!

An ELEPHANT & PIGGIE Book

Hyperion Books for Children / *New York*

AN IMPRINT OF DISNEY BOOK GROUP

Piggie!

I have a great idea!

If we are going on a drive—

we need a plan!

A plan?

9

17

Bringing sunglasses on a drive is smart planning.

21

24

Make a plan and
stick to it, is what I say.

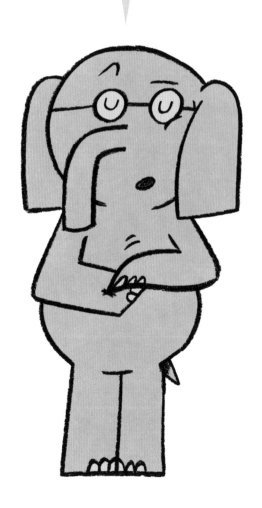

28

32

35

37